Best Sleepover Club Friends!

Have you been invited to all these sleepovers?

The Sleepover Club Best Friends

The Sleepover Club TV Stars

The Sleepover Club Dance-off!

The Sleepover Club Hit the Beach!

Coming soon...

The Sleepover Club Pet Detectives

The Sleepover Club Hey Baby!

Best

The Sleepover Club

Friends!

Rose Impey

HarperCollins *Children's Books*

The Sleepover Club ® is a registered trademark
of HarperCollins*Publishers* Ltd

First published in Great Britain by HarperCollins *Children's Books* in 2008
HarperCollins *Children's Books* is a division of HarperCollins*Publishers* Ltd,
77–85 Fulham Palace Road, Hammersmith, London W6 8JB

www.harpercollinschildrensbooks.co.uk

2

ISBN-13 978-0-00-726494-0
ISBN-10 0-00-726494-1

Printed and bound in England by
Clays Ltd, St Ives plc

Mixed Sources
Product group from well-managed
forests and other controlled sources
www.fsc.org   Cert no. SW-COC-1806
© 1996 Forest Stewardship Council

FSC is a non-profit international organisation established to promote the
responsible management of the world's forests. Products carrying the FSC
label are independently certified to assure consumers that they come
from forests that are managed to meet the social, economic and
ecological needs of present and future generations.

Find out more about HarperCollins and the environment at
www.harpercollins.co.uk/green

The Sleepover Kit List

1. Sleeping bag
2. Pillow
3. Pyjamas or a nightdress
4. Slippers
5. Toothbrush, toothpaste, soap etc
6. Towel
7. Teddy
8. A creepy story
9. Food for a midnight feast: chocolate, crisps, sweets, biscuits. Anything you like to eat!
10. Torch
11. Hairbrush
12. Hair bobble or hairband, if you need them
13. Change of clothes for the next day
14. Sleepover diary and membership card

1

Hey, pssst. It's me, Frankie – over here, in the bushes. Don't look round! And whatever you do, *don't* look up! Meet me the other side of the dog park in five. I'll be the one in the sunglasses and the mad hat. And come alone – this is for your ears only!

Sorry about the cloak and dagger stuff, but this time it's serious. This time we almost got arrested. And we still might – if this rescue operation goes wrong. I'm dreading it. You know what I'm like about heights!

Anyway, let's find somewhere to sit while we're waiting for the others and I'll tell you the whole gory story...

Now, where shall I start? I probably need to go way back, before the Sleepover Club even existed and tell you how we all came to be best friends – *and sworn enemies of the gruesome M&Ms.*

In the very beginning there were just two of us: Me, Francesca Theresa Thomas – Frankie to all my friends (which of course means you) – and my best mate Kenny. Her real name's Laura McKenzie, but everyone calls her Kenny – if they know what's good for them! We met at playschool when we were three years old. Kenny came flying down the slide and smashed right into the back of me. I was so mad, until I saw her cheeky grin and heard her say, "Hey, soz, didn't see you there," which was pretty unbelievable, because even then I was big for my age. But I couldn't stay angry with Kenny for long and it's been like that ever since.

Sometimes in drama lessons we do this exercise where we have to describe a character we're playing as if they're a piece of fruit or… a piece of furniture. For example, if I were a piece of furniture, I'd be this *a-mazing* chair I once saw in a museum. It looked Egyptian; it was like a huge throne, with carved wooden legs with cats' heads on them. It wasn't what you'd call comfortable, but *dead cool*. I would kill to have it in my bedroom.

Kenny would be a chair too, but one of those office chairs. You know, the type that goes up and down and round in circles and given the slightest encouragement charges across the room at forty miles an hour skittling everything in its path. It would be blue and white, which are Leicester City Football Club colours, because Kenny is their biggest fan. And it would probably be waving a scarf and cheering!

We met Lyndz, Lyndsey Collins, when we were five and went to Cuddington County Primary School. If Lyndz were a chair she'd be soft and cozy, the most comfy armchair in the world. Imagine your favourite place to cuddle up and watch TV, or read a book – that's Lyndz.

I know everyone says threes don't work – someone's bound to end up left out and feeling jealous – but Lyndz doesn't have a jealous bone in her body so we all got on just fine. In class, if ever we had to work in pairs, Lyndz would choose some Billy-no-mates to work with. Lyndz has this big heart, so big you could probably float the whole of Leicester on it.

One of the people she sometimes took pity on was Fliss, full name: Felicity Diana Sidebotham. Fliss is definitely not a chair. She'd be more like one of those fancy curved dressing tables. You know the kind, with pink curtains underneath and frills and tassels. Fliss is a very pink person.

It's hard to imagine now, but in those days she was a bit of a Felicity-no-mates. She was a bit shy and a bit *girly* for Kenny's taste. But when the M&Ms started their Campaign of

Terror, well, we had to do something, didn't we?

The M&Ms' real names are Emma Hughes and Emily Berryman – sometimes known as The Queen and the Goblin or The Gruesome Twosome. The M&Ms would have been our enemies, even if they'd never done anything to us, just because they're the most disgusting, sneaky, stuck up goody-goodies in the entire history of the universe and beyond. And, no, I'm not exaggerating!

If the M&Ms were pieces of furniture they'd probably be matching gold mirrors, like the one in Snow White. If you asked them, "Who is the fairest of us all?" they'd scream back at you, "We are, of course, you idiot!"

One of the most irritating things about the M&Ms is that they always have to be top of everything and bosses of the class. If there's ever a competition with a prize to win, somehow they *always* manage to win it.

But worse than that: their idea of fun is to pick on people who can't stick up for themselves. And one of those people was Fliss.

Fliss *really* cares about her appearance and – how can I put this – well, she's pretty vain. So, when the M&Ms stuck chewing gum in her long blonde hair, squirted tomato ketchup – accidentally on purpose – down her designer T-shirt and put hamster droppings in the pocket of her new, very expensive Bennetton jacket… and then squashed them, Fliss almost had a nervous breakdown.

As if all that wasn't enough, they started to give her the Smile Treatment. Believe me, there is nothing more unpleasant than being smiled at by those two muppets. Whenever Fliss glanced up from her work one of them was already looking in her direction, *smiling*. She'd nudge the other one and they'd both smile, as if to say, "Wait till you see what we've got planned for you!"

In no time Fliss was a complete designer bag of nerves. Her mum, Nicky, told us later she'd been having trouble getting Fliss to school for weeks. She'd even threatened to run away which was a big thing for Fliss, because camping is on her list of Least Favourite Things to do Before I Die.

Anyway, when Lyndz found her crying one day in the toilets at school she came straight back and told us.

"I think we should let Fliss sit with us in class," she said. "I feel *sooo*…"

"…*sorry for her*," Kenny and I joined in. That could be Lyndz's theme tune.

"Well, I do," she insisted.

At first, we weren't exactly sympathetic, because as Kenny said, "It doesn't take a lot to get Fliss crying." But once we'd heard the full list of things those two gonks had been up to, even Kenny said, "OK, now I feel sorry for her."

So for the next week the four of us sat together in lessons and it was OK. If any bits of bother broke out between Kenny and Fliss, Lyndz launched one of her international peace-keeping missions. In fact everything seemed fine until Fliss turned up to school with *the invitations*. I bet you can guess what colour those were!

Lyndz opened hers first and broke out into a big smile, so then I opened mine. I thought it would just be an invitation to tea, but it was for tea… *and* to sleep over… at Fliss's house… all four of us.

Lyndz looked pretty pleased; I was… surprised; Kenny was trying not to choke. I mean, we'd never really done anything like that before. Kenny had slept at my house once or twice, and I'd stayed once at Lyndz's when my parents went to a conference, but we'd never had a *proper* sleepover – not all of us together.

As Kenny said later, "We don't really *know* Fliss yet."

We'd never even been to her house. We weren't sure we were ready for this. But Lyndz said, "I think we should go. It'll be… nice."

"It'll be *pink*," Kenny muttered.

"Come on, it'll be fun," Lyndz persisted.

"It'll be *frilly*," Kenny argued.

They both turned and looked at me. "What do you think, Frankie?"

If I'm absolutely honest, which is what my parents always encourage me to be, because they're lawyers and they think honesty is *more important than anything else in life*, I'd probably have to admit I was on Kenny's side. I don't like change much. I thought we were fine as we were, just the three of us. It wasn't that I had anything against *Fliss* joining our gang, I didn't want *anyone* to join.

The others were waiting for me to give the casting vote, but before I could the M&Ms came round the corner and saw the invitations in our hands.

"Oooh, someone's having a party," Emma Hughes said in her silly, simpery voice.

"It wouldn't be Flossy *Slidebottom*, would it?" Emily Berryman asked.

"She must be desperate for friends if she's got to ask *this* lot," Emma sneered.

15

"At least she's *got* some friends," I snapped back at them.

"Not just partners in crime," Kenny backed me up.

The M&Ms grinned at each other like they'd won some points for how easily they could wind us up.

"Well, have a *wonderful* time," Emma Hughes simpered as they disappeared down the corridor.

"Oh, we will!" I called after them.

"Don't you worry," Kenny added. "We'll have a ball!"

"We'll have the best time *ever*," I shouted even louder.

After they'd gone Lyndz stood there, trying not to smile.

"I take it we're going then," she said.

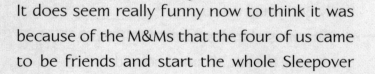

It does seem really funny now to think it was because of the M&Ms that the four of us came to be friends and start the whole Sleepover

Club in the first place. It's what my gran calls *poetic justice*.

"Sometimes," she says, "really good things can come – even out of the most unlikely places!"

Fliss was so excited when we accepted her invitations it made us all feel pretty mean. She must have asked fifty times what kind of food we liked to eat and did two of us mind sleeping in sleeping bags on the floor. "Because I've only got two beds, but Mum's bought these cool new duvet covers. They're the most fantastic colour..."

I could see Kenny rolling her eyes and mouthing, "Pink!"

I thought it would be a bit of a miracle if we actually got Kenny there on the Friday, but in the end we all made it.

As my mum and dad dropped us off they said, "Have a great time."

"And try to get some sleep," Mum added.

I told her, "That's why it's called a *sleep*over, Mum, because that's what you do!"

"If only it worked like that," Mum sighed, which just goes to show that sometimes mums know more than you think!

From the moment Nicky opened the door and we got our first glimpse of Fliss's house, we all started to worry.

If Fliss is a pink person, her mum, Nicky, is pale cream. Don't get me wrong, Nicky's great, we love her to bits – now we know her. But when she asked us to take off our shoes before we came in and check our bags were clean before we put them down on the carpet we knew we'd have to be on our best behaviour.

She led us straight through to her shiny

cream kitchen where she'd set out this tea party. The table was covered with little cakes and jellies and miniature sandwiches and rolls, and there were balloons and streamers and candles, like it was this full-on birthday party or something, just for the four of us! Fliss's younger brother, Callum, was there, of course, staring at us like we were three aliens who'd come to tea. But Kenny did that cross-eyed thing she does which soon stopped him.

You could see Nicky was feeling pretty nervous and it was making all of us nervous too. We're not exactly clumsy types but we kept nudging each other as we reached for the same sandwich.

"Ooops, sorry," Lyndz said.

"No, my fault," I insisted.

Then Kenny knocked her drink over! It was like it was in slow motion: the juice flew up in the air but Kenny followed it with her cup and did this brilliant save, managing to catch every drop. It was such a great party trick we all felt like cheering. But Nicky clearly didn't realise how fast Kenny's reflexes are, because she looked like she might faint with the tension.

Then Lyndz slurped her drink, which she often does. But the room was so quiet the slurp sounded like it was on loudspeaker. We couldn't wait to finish tea and escape upstairs to Fliss's bedroom. But when we finally did – can you believe it – Nicky came with us!

She sat on Fliss's bed, smiling. "Why don't you show your friends round a bit," she suggested. So Fliss gave us a guided tour of her wardrobes – yes, she has two! Then her drawers with all her clothes colour coordinated

"These are my second best tops and T-shirts," she said, "but these…" she added, opening another cupboard, "are my very best. For special occasions only." They were neatly folded like they have them in the shops. Some were still in plastic covers to keep them perfectly clean.

We all knew Fliss was mad about clothes, but until then we hadn't realised it was like a religion with her. I could see Kenny looking for the nearest exit and when Nicky suggested to Fliss we might want to play some games next, I thought I might join her.

I had a horrible feeling Nicky might have made us a Pin the Tail on the Donkey and we'd spend the whole night pretending to have a really, spiffing, jolly time. Even Fliss was feeling embarrassed by now.

"Actually, Mum," she said, "I think we might just sit and… talk for a bit."

"OK," Nicky said, brightly, but just went on sitting there!

Fliss screwed her face up and said, "Mu-u-um…" until Nicky finally got the hint.

"I'll just leave you to it then, shall I?" she said, closing the door.

We'd all just let out our breath for the first time since we arrived when she was suddenly back. "But let me know if there's anything you need. I could bring you a drink in half an hour when you're ready for bed."

Half an hour! She had to be joking.

"We'll let you know, Mum," Fliss said between gritted teeth, firmly closing the door behind her.

Even after we heard Nicky's footsteps going downstairs we went on sitting there, feeling really awkward. And then a terrible thing happened: Fliss burst into tears.

"Oh, it's been horrible, hasn't it?" she sobbed. "You've all hated it. You'll never come again. You won't be my friends any more. I don't blame you; nobody likes me!"

This was far worse than anything that had happened so far. Kenny and I didn't know what to do. But good old Lyndz went and sat beside Fliss and put her arm round her.

"Don't be silly," she said. "It's been... lovely. We don't know each other very well yet; it's bound to be a bit awkward the first time."

Kenny and I tried not to look like we were thinking: *you can say that again.*

And then Lyndz's next suggestion had us both ready to bolt.

"I know a little game we could play," she said.

"What kind of game?" Kenny asked suspiciously.

"We'll need a pen and a sheet of paper each. We fold the paper into a fan and we put our name on it," Lyndz told us.

"Then what?" I asked, equally suspiciously.

"We pass the fan round and everyone has to write something nice on it, something they like about us. They're called friendship fans…" Lyndz trailed off. She was looking at me, sort of appealingly.

In the end I just shrugged and said, "OK, why not?"

I didn't look at Kenny. I knew she'd have plenty of reasons why not if I gave her half a chance. But afterwards even Kenny had to admit it was actually a fun thing to do, because everyone had something nice or funny or *surprising* written about them.

Everyone told Lyndz what a good laugh and a great person she was and how we even loved her smiley knees, which she has a thing about – and her hiccups, which she gets all the time!

I'm not being bigheaded, but I got lots of comments about being a good leader and having all the best ideas and being the person everyone would want with them if they were ever stranded on a desert island – you know the kind of stuff.

But most surprising were the things Fliss and Kenny wrote about each other.

Kenny said she thought Fliss was *a bit of a genius* when it came to colours and clothes and things. And while she didn't give a stuff about them most of the time herself it would probably be good to have Fliss's talent – in case you ever needed it.

And Fliss wrote how Kenny was her *all-time hero*. She said she thought Kenny was the bravest, most fearless person she'd ever met and she really wanted to be more like her, instead of being scared of everything. She said she couldn't believe someone like Kenny would want to be friends with someone like her.

When Kenny heard that she went very…*pink*

and did what she always does when she's embarrassed: started pulling ridiculous faces and behaving like an idiot until she had us all rolling around on the floor in hysterics.

That completely broke the ice. Then things just got better and better and the sleepover really got going.

3

Can you remember your first sleepover? It's always special, isn't it? Sort of the best. Well, this one started off the worst – but then it was *the best*. A lot of the things that we do now whenever we have our sleepovers, we thought up that first night.

International Gladiators was Kenny's idea and, because it was Kenny's idea, Fliss was determined to give it a go. She wanted to prove she wasn't a wimp and could be pretty fearless too.

The first event Kenny came up with was called Barging Contests. We have to get into pairs, one on the other's back, like we're horse riding. The two riders have to try to knock each other off using only their elbows, or sometimes a squishy pooh. A squishy pooh can be a sleeping bag, or a pillow case filled with clothes or cushions, that you swing at your opponent trying to knock her off. It can be pretty wild, especially when Kenny's on the other end of the squishy pooh.

Having seen Fliss's bedroom, I never thought she'd go for it in a gazillion years. She has enough ornaments and toys around to open a shop. But in minutes she'd cleared everything breakable out of the way and was on Lyndz's back ready to do battle.

"Let's go, go, go!" she squealed, hanging on to Lyndz for dear life and whirling her squishy pooh around her head.

"Prepare to meet the floor!" Kenny warned her.

"You wish," Fliss replied.

I've probably made Fliss sound a bit of a fuss-pot (which she can be) and a bit of a cry baby (which she used to be), but Fliss is lots of other things too. She can be *fierce* when it's a competition; she loves to win as much as Kenny does, and she really gave her a run for her money.

"Bulls eye!" Fliss shrieked every time she caught Kenny off guard. If Kenny wasn't so tough Fliss would have had her off loads of times. I knew how hard Kenny was trying by the way she was digging her heels into me. Kenny's such a brilliant aim, she hardly ever misses, but Fliss was brilliant too – at ducking. Several times Kenny missed her completely and nearly fell off herself.

In fact Fliss was doing so well she started getting cocky. Big mistake.

"So who's got a date with the floor?" Fliss asked grinning, and forgetting to duck.

Wham! Kenny caught her full in the face. She fell backwards on to the bed carrying her horse with her. The pair of them landed so heavily the whole house seemed to shake.

In moments Nicky burst into the room expecting to find one of us fatally injured. Instead she found Fliss and Lyndz lying on the bed with their legs in the air, screaming with laughter.

"It's OK, Mum, don't get your knickers in a twist," Fliss told her. "Nobody broke anything."

"I think you won," Fliss told Kenny afterwards.

But Kenny admitted, "It was a close thing."

After our mad half hour we thought we'd perhaps better quieten down a bit and at least start getting ready for bed. Then we all suddenly got a bit shy around each other again, so Fliss said we could get undressed in the bathroom. But Lyndz said, "No need," and she taught us all this brilliant technique she called Sleeping Bag Striptease.

"This is what you do," she said, wriggling down inside her sleeping bag until only her head was poking out, and started flinging her clothes out around the room and finally pulling on her PJs. Then she sat up looking a bit hot and bothered, but grinning from ear to ear.

When we timed ourselves, Kenny was the fastest, even though it was the first time she'd ever done it. But Fliss was almost as fast.

That twenty seconds record that Kenny set has been beaten lots of times since. Not by me, I might add, because I'm too tall. There's never as much room in my sleeping bag and I often end up with both legs down the same trouser leg. It's not easy being a beanpole, you know.

Once we were all ready for bed came the best part: the midnight feast. We'd all brought secret supplies and, after we were quite sure Nicky wasn't coming back in, we turned off all the lights and sat round in a circle with our torches on. Kenny said we should put all the food together in a bowl that we'd made Fliss sneak down to the kitchen to borrow.

"You can't possibly mix smoky bacon crisps with Skittles and fruit jellies," Fliss said, horrified.

"Watch me," Kenny said, busy tearing packets open.

Then we passed the bowl round and all tucked in. It was a bit like a lucky dip, not knowing what you'd pull out. Afterwards the crumbs and stuff left in the bottom did look a bit of a mess: "Like Nappy's brain," I said.

There's a really annoying boy who lives next door to me, called Nathan, but I call him Nappyhead. If he had a brain, which I doubt, it would probably look just like that bowl of mangled leftovers.

"Somebody should eat it," Kenny said, grinning. "I dare Lyndz."

But before Lyndz had chance to say anything, Fliss said, "I'll do it," and stuffed her mouth full to bursting, while the rest of us made being sick noises.

"Whoa! Way to go, Fliss," Lyndz said and we all cheered. There was definitely more to Fliss than we'd realised.

Although it was getting really late by now

no one wanted to get into bed and go to sleep.

"Tell us a story, Frankie," Kenny said.

"What kind of story?"

"Scary," said Lyndz, grinning, "at least a *bit* scary."

"Yeah, full of blood and guts," Kenny said, drawing her top lip back and baring her teeth so she looked like a vampire.

But being scared half to death in her own bedroom was not one of the things Fliss was up for. "I don't do scary," she said firmly. "I'll have nightmares."

"Not with us here, you won't," Kenny promised. Famous last words.

While the other two sat right beside her with their arms round her shoulders, I made up this story about a bloodsucking vampire called Vladimir that lives at the top of the Clock Tower in the middle of Leicester.

"He can make himself invisible so he can slip into your bags and follow you home when you've been shopping," I told them.

"Don't say that," Fliss begged. "I'm always

round there shopping with my mum. I'll never dare go again," she wailed.

"For goodness sake, it's a story," Kenny said. "Get on with it, Frankie."

"One day he slipped into the shopping bag of a girl called F-f-f…"

"Oh, don't make it Fliss," she begged.

"*Fiona*," I said. "When she got home Fiona opened her shopping to show her sister and little did she realise that the vampire had slipped out unseen into her bedroom, waiting for his moment to re-materialise."

While I was telling the story I shone my torch under my chin and grinned, which Fliss said made me look really spooky and a bit like a vampire.

"Later," I went on, "when the girl was lying in bed, all on her own, Vladimir slid over and sank his long vampire's teeth into her soft white neck…"

When I looked over at Fliss she was holding on to her own neck as if she thought the vampire was in the room with us. By the time I'd finished even Lyndz was looking a bit sick.

Kenny, of course, was grinning from ear to ear. She loves talking about blood so much I sometimes think she might have been a vampire herself in a previous life.

But Fliss was really nervous. Before she would get into bed we had to pull out every shopping bag she owned and turn it inside out. Even then she couldn't relax.

"He could still be here," she insisted, "if he was invisible."

"It was a *story*," Kenny reminded her again.

"Honest, I just made it all up," I promised her.

But we had to go on sitting there for a while in a huddle telling jokes, even though we were all so tired we were dying to get into bed.

By the time we finally settled down we'd already heard two o'clock strike on the hall clock downstairs. I was just dropping off when I heard Fliss whisper, "Is anyone still awake?"

"Mumph," Lyndz sort of grunted.

"Yeah," I said, although I wasn't really.

"What now?" Kenny asked grumpily.

"I hope you've all had a good time," Fliss said in this tiny little voice.

"You bet," said Lyndz, yawning. "I think we should do it again."

No one said anything for a moment. I knew it had been fun but I wasn't sure how keen Kenny would be, after all the reservations she'd had in the first place.

"*Maybe*," I said tentatively.

But suddenly Kenny's torch snapped on and she was sitting up in bed, saying, "Are you joking?! This was my best night *ever*. Sleepovers really rock. I think we should do it again next weekend… and the weekend after that."

"And the weekend after that…" said Lyndz, yawning.

"And the weekend after…" was the last thing I heard as I finally fell asleep.

The next morning we were so tired and sleepy we all got a bit of an ear-wigging from our parents. We thought it probably wasn't the best time to break the news to them that this was going to be like *a regular thing* from now on.

So, although we have to give some of the responsibility for Sleepover Club to the gruesome M&Ms, a lot of it has to go to Fliss too. If she hadn't invited us to that first one, and been prepared to have a really mad time – even in her perfect pink bedroom – who knows what would have happened.

Back then we had no idea where it would all lead – how absolutely *fantabuloso* the Sleepover Club was going to be. Or that quite soon we'd have a fifth and final member, someone we hadn't even met yet.

Please welcome: Rosie Cartwright.

We had three more sleepovers that summer, one at each of our houses. Kenny's was the last, not because her parents minded, but because Molly the Monster did! Kenny has to share a bedroom with her evil older sister. I'll tell you all about her another time.

Now that she really feels she's one of us, Fliss likes to pretend the *whole thing* was her idea. But it was me who suggested we make it official and actually call ourselves The

Sleepover Club. And it was at the sleepover at my house we first decided to keep sleepover diaries and make our first membership cards. They weren't flashy, with photos, like we have now, but that's where it started.

One time we made the mistake of letting the M&Ms catch a glimpse of them, and we never heard the end of it.

"Ooooh, they're a proper club now," Emma Hughes sneered. "How cute. What's it called?"

"The Losers' Club?" suggested Emily Berryman.

"Well, they'll all get life membership to that one," Emma sniggered.

We never worked out how, because we wouldn't have breathed a word to those two gonks, but they soon got to know all about our sleepovers. Even though they kept making pathetic jokes about it, you could tell they were pea-green with envy. And guess what? In no time they were planning sleepovers of their own. But apart from soppy Alana Palmer – or

Alana Banana as we call her – the M&Ms couldn't find anyone else to hang out with. Certainly no one who'd want to spend a whole night in the same room as them.

So, when Rosie Cartwright joined our school, they were buzzing round her like wasps round a jam pot.

Rosie and her family had moved into the big house at the end of Welby Drive during the summer holidays. It had a massive garden and an orchard. When the FOR SALE sign came down we were all a bit curious to find out who'd moved in. Then, when school started back, Rosie was suddenly there – in our class.

She seemed a bit shy at first and kept to herself, but we thought she looked pretty cool. The best thing about her, though, was that she seemed to know straight off that the M&Ms were trouble and to keep well clear of them. That didn't stop them from following her around, though, cornering her in the corridors, trying to find out all about her.

"We *love* your house," we overheard Emma Hughes telling her.

"We've been dying to see who'd move in," agreed Emily Berryman. "How many rooms does it have?"

"My house has eleven," Emma bragged, "but we're planning a loft conversion. Then I shall have my own bedroom – with *en suite* – which will be perfect for *sleepovers*."

"What's *your* bedroom like?" Emily asked.

Rosie didn't seem to want to talk about it. As we found out later, although it was a big house, it was very run down. It was a while before we got to see inside and hear what had happened. Rosie's dad's a builder and before they moved in he'd completely stripped it out ready to do it up. But two weeks later he moved out, leaving her mum for someone else. Rosie said half the walls were just bare plaster, including her room. If she'd told the M&Ms that, they'd have probably screwed up their noses and run a mile screaming, "Bare plaster! Eeewww!"

It wasn't long before Lyndz was feeling *a bit sorry for* Rosie, especially when the locusts descended. She claimed Rosie had given her this desperate look that said, "Save me, please!" So in no time Rosie was sitting with us in class *and* she'd joined our Brownie pack.

To tell you the truth, I wasn't quite sure about it at first. Like I already told you, I don't like change. Even after Lyndz invited Rosie to one of our sleepovers, *one at my house*, I still wasn't sure about her.

Apparently she had a few doubts about us, she told us later! She thought *we* were weird! Can you believe it? But then something happened that changed my mind about Rosie Cartwright – in fact it changed *everything* really.

One Friday afternoon, a couple of weeks into the term, our teacher, Mrs Weaver, made an announcement. She'd been telling us all week how disappointed she was with our work so far. "It seems to me that after your long summer holidays, some of you have left your brains behind on the beach. I think everyone needs to shape up a bit – give those brains a good kick-start. And I think I've come up with an idea of how to do that."

We all looked at the teacher, wondering what she'd got in mind. We really liked Mrs Weaver, but we hoped it wasn't going to be more tests; they were always so boring. But her new idea wasn't.

"We're going to have a competition," she announced, "to find out who can learn the most facts in a week."

"A week?" everyone complained. "That's not long."

"That's the point," she told us. "You'll be working under pressure. So let's see who rises to the challenge – and who doesn't. Who are the slow-coaches that are sleepwalking through the term? Who's running out of steam? Who needs a tiger in their tank? We're going to discover who are the Weakest Links and vote them off until we finally have *a winner*."

"Will there be a prize, Mrs Weaver?" Emma Hughes immediately wanted to know.

"There certainly will," Mrs Weaver said, smiling and waving a shiny silver cup in the air that she'd been hiding behind her back. "So put on those thinking caps and get those brains into gear. Let's see who's the fastest and who's the cleverest because it's countdown to the Cup!"

Well, that set the M&Ms off. You'd have thought she'd held up the crown jewels. Their eyes were almost sticking out of their heads on stalks. Whenever the M&Ms hear words like "fastest" and "cleverest" alarm bells go off inside their heads screaming: *Me! Me! Me! Me! Me! Me! Me!*

"It's a pity there's only one cup," we heard Emma Hughes telling Emily Berryman later. "I suppose we'll have to take it in turns, a week each."

"You've got to win it first," Kenny couldn't resist reminding them.

"And who's going to stop us? You and the Losers' Club? I don't think so."

That made us really mad; until then we'd only ever had minor scraps with the M&Ms, but all that was about to change – as soon as they realised that we had a secret weapon and it was called *Rosie Cartwright*.

We had no idea that Rosie would turn out to have the largest collection of useless information in her head of anyone we had ever met. We found out later that afternoon when we had a practice run. Mrs Weaver kept throwing out questions and Rosie just knocked them down like skittles. No one else got a look in.

Mrs Weaver: Who led the first expedition to the South Pole?

Rosie: Amundsen.

Mrs Weaver: After which Norse god is the day Thursday named?

Rosie: Thor.

Mrs Weaver: What is the name of the giant tapestry that tells the story of the Norman Invasion of England?

Rosie: The Bayeux Tapestry.

Mrs Weaver: How many syllables are there in a haiku?

Rosie: Seventeen.

Now, listen, I don't want you thinking I was in the least bit jealous of Rosie, because I wasn't. No! I wasn't! It was just that I knew those answers – well, some of them – but I hardly had time to get my hand up, because she was so fast.

Finally Mrs Weaver said, "Now here's a harder one: Do stalactites or stalagmites hang down from the roofs of caves?"

Oh, oh, oh, I knew this, but before I could get the words out of my mouth Rosie had already said, "Stalactites."

"Correct! My word, whichever team you join is going to take some beating, Rosie." Then Mrs Weaver reminded us, "This is going to be a team effort. Everyone will play their part, collecting questions and pooling the information they find. Before next Friday each team will choose their two strongest players to represent them. Remember, each person will be playing for their team as well as themselves."

Finally she told us that a team should be made up of five people, which was perfect for us – provided Rosie was part of our team.

"How come you know all that stuff?" Kenny whispered to her afterwards.

Rosie shrugged. "Years of playing *Trivial Pursuit*," she explained. "If you think I'm good, you should meet Adam. I've never beaten him yet."

Adam is Rosie's brother. He has cerebral palsy and can't speak, except through an electronic voice machine. Sometimes he head spells, which is quicker and really neat. He's dead competitive too and Rosie says his favourite thing is beating her at quiz games. She says if *Trivial Pursuit* was an Olympic event, Adam would get the gold.

The M&Ms couldn't wait for school to finish to corner Rosie and try to get her on their team. First they tried a bit of gentle persuasion, and when that didn't work they tried bribery and bullying.

We stood nearby watching. Rosie knew that everyone wanted her on our team – at least all the others did; I still wasn't sure. But unlike the Gruesome Twosome, we weren't putting any pressure on her. OK, so maybe Fliss was jumping up and down on the spot and hissing under her breath: *"Choose us! Choose us!"* But that's not the same.

When the M&Ms finished their sales pitch, Rosie said, very sweetly, "No. I'm really sorry I'm already in a team, thanks all the same."

Ha! The M&Ms looked like they'd won the lottery and lost their ticket. As we all walked off home together they could see their chances of winning the cup disappearing down the road with us.

We didn't know it yet, but from the word "No" the M&Ms had started planning their dirty tricks campaign.

We'd decided to hit the ground running and agreed to meet at my house on the weekend to start practising. I tried to swing a sleepover but my parents still hadn't got over the last one: the Brown Owl Fiasco. It was completely crazy. I'll tell you all about it another time.

So Saturday afternoon, while the rest of us surfed the Internet or flicked through encyclopedias, collecting possible questions, Fliss sat cross-legged on my bed, humming and sewing some long pieces of ribbon together. Yes, you guessed it: pink!

Kenny and I looked over at her and shook our heads.

"This isn't a sewing circle, you know, Fliss," Kenny told her. "There's important work to be done here." And she waved a book of animal facts under her nose.

"I know that," Fliss said, pushing the book away. "We all have our jobs, Kenny, and mine is to make sure that our team is at least colour coordinated." She held up one of the sashes she was busy making for us to wear. Then she riffled through her bag and pulled out a matching bear.

"Meet Bubbles…" she said proudly "…our team mascot."

"He's bright *pink*!" Kenny almost choked, but Lyndz gave her a quick slap on the back.

"Yes, and he's a very special bear," Fliss said fondly. "I just know he's going to bring us luck."

We all smiled and rolled our eyes. We were thinking: *who needs luck, with Rosie Cartwright on our team?* But then we hadn't realised what new levels the M&Ms were prepared to stoop to.

On Monday we soon found out.

5

At school on Monday morning, as soon as the M&Ms saw our mascot they started smirking and whispering and giving us all the Smile Treatment.

Oh, yuk!

"Just ignore them," Lyndz kept saying, and we did manage to – well, most of us did. I had to keep Kenny on a short lead or she would probably have gone over there and hit them over the head with Bubbles.

Our last lesson was PE and when we went outside Fliss left Bubbles on her desk. When we came back in, he was gone and we didn't have to look far to know who'd got him.

We didn't tell Mrs Weaver – *obviously* – the Sleepover Club don't snitch. We knew what the M&Ms were up to: just trying to distract us. Anyway, even those gonks would have to give him back some time. We were determined we wouldn't let them see they'd rattled us.

That night we all worked even harder, ringing each other up and asking random questions.

"At what age did Mozart compose his first work?" I asked Rosie.

"Five years old," she said. "What's the longest river in the world?" she asked me.

"The Amazon," I said proudly.

"Nope, that's the second," she said. "The longest's the Nile."

Rats! I still hadn't found one to catch her out, not even when I asked her: "Which US president are teddy bears named after?"

"Oh, too easy," she said. "Teddy Roosevelt."

Later I asked my parents to give me a couple of really hard ones.

"Who crowned Napoleon emperor of France?" Dad asked.

"I don't know. The Pope?"

"No one. He crowned himself," Dad said, smiling. "Where would you be if a step in any direction would take you south?"

"That sounds like another trick question," I said.

"They all *seem* like trick questions – if you don't know the answers," Mum told me, which was very helpful, NOT!

(The answer, by the way, is the North Pole.)

Just before I went to bed I rang Rosie; I was sure I'd got her this time. "What unusual pet did Julius Caesar have?" I asked.

"Giraffe," she said as if everyone and her auntie knew that fact.

"See you in the morning, brainbox," I said and pulled a face, which luckily she couldn't see over the phone.

The following day, when we went into school and found Bubbles was still missing, we decided to tackle the gruesome M&Ms.

"OK, what have you done with him?" Kenny demanded.

"Yes, where's Bubbles?" I added.

But they both did this thing where they made their eyes stick out and tried to look as if butter wouldn't melt in their mouths.

"Why would *we* know anything about your pathetic mascot?" they said, turning their backs and walking off.

"OK, if that's how they want to play it," Fliss declared, rolling up her sleeves. "But I hope they're ready for a fight."

After that, beating the M&Ms became a matter of honour, especially for Fliss.

After school we'd arranged to go round to Lyndz's to practise some more. It was a good excuse to hang out together. We were all up in

Lyndz's tree house. I *know* I told you I don't like heights, but the others didn't know that and I wasn't going to tell them.

Lyndz's dad made the tree house for her older brothers, Stuart and Tom. Now they're almost grown up they never use it, so it's Lyndz's. We don't go up there very often because Fliss finds it pretty scary, which saves me having to admit that heights give *me* the creeps too. It's bad enough being that far off the ground, but if there's any wind it sways and I start to get sort of up-in-the-air sickness.

Anyway, the reason we were up there was because it was literally the only quiet place we could find. Lyndz's dad was putting up a new ceiling in the kitchen and her four brothers were all home: the older two helping their dad and the younger two getting in the way.

Although we were supposed to be preparing for the quiz, we were mostly talking about our next sleepover, which wasn't going to be happening any time soon. Like I told you, we were all still in deep doom with our parents over the last one.

Rosie and Lyndz kept throwing out questions but I couldn't seem to concentrate. It wasn't only because Rosie was getting them all right, as usual, and leaving no time for me to think. I was busy watching Kenny, too. She was scanning the skyline through Lyndz's dad's binoculars and I kept wondering how she could stand that near the edge and not need to hold on to anything.

"*Ohmygod!*" she suddenly yelled. "Hey, Lyndz, did you know you can see into Emily Berryman's back garden from here?"

"Would I want to?" was Lyndz's reply.

"They're practising too, by the look of it," Kenny told us. Then she described the scene: the M&Ms were sitting behind a table, covered with big books, probably encyclopedias, with their own mascot between them. Kenny said it was a fat brown bear, nearly as big as my bear, Stanley.

"They've got a nerve," Fliss growled.

Alana Banana was asking them questions

and, according to Kenny, every time they got an answer right they high-fived, waved their mascot in the air and then threw a handful of... something that looked like peanuts across the garden. Even for the M&Ms that sounded pretty weird behaviour.

"Let me see," Fliss demanded, holding out her hand for the binoculars.

"It's true," she said. "What are they aiming at?"

Whatever the target was, it was just out of view. Kenny took back the binoculars.

"Hang on to me, Frankie," she ordered. "I'm going to find out."

I had to swallow my nerves and grab the waistband of Kenny's jeans to make sure she didn't completely disappear while she hung like a monkey halfway out of the tree house. That way she finally managed to see the rest of the garden.

"Kenny, come back," Fliss pleaded. "What if you fall?"

"Oh–you–are–never–going–to–believe–this!" Kenny announced.

"What? What?" Fliss squealed.

"Pull us in, Frankie," she demanded, and I hauled her back to safety.

Then she stood there, grinning in that infuriating way she has, saying nothing until we all screamed at her: *"What!"*

She finally told us what – or rather *who* - they were throwing the peanuts at: *Bubbles!*

"Bubbles!" shrieked Fliss. "Those maggots! I am going to kill them."

But that wasn't all. Kenny said they'd tied poor Bubbles to a chair and hung a big sign round his neck saying: LOSER!

It took all four of us to calm Fliss down when she heard that. She looked like she might launch herself through the air and parachute down into Emily Berryman's garden to rescue him – only she probably wouldn't bother with the parachute.

"OK, calm down," I told her, taking control. "Don't worry, we'll get him back. We just need a rescue plan. We need to split up," I said, thinking fast on my feet. "Some of us have to get the M&Ms out of their garden long enough for the rest of us to go in, grab Bubbles, and get out before they come back."

But how to draw the M&Ms away? That was the question. Then I had this brilliant idea. Emma Hughes has this swanky new turquoise bike. She goes everywhere on it. We'd actually seen it just inside the gate at Emily Berryman's house as we'd walked past on the way home from school.

"Kenny and I will sneak round there," I told the others, "grab the bike and take it a few streets away. Then we'll ring the M&Ms and tell them we just happen to have found it…"

"Then they'll come and get it back…" Kenny continued.

"Leaving the coast clear for the rest of you…" I said, pretty proud of my plan.

"You lot go in, bag the bear and beat it, pronto," Kenny told the others. "Great plan, *amigo*," she grinned at me.

"Thanks," I said as we high-fived.

"You mean you're going to *steal* her bike?" Lyndz said, clearly not as impressed with the plan as we were.

"Not *steal* it," I corrected her.

"We're going to *find it* for her," Kenny grinned.

"It isn't actually lost, though, is it," Fliss pointed out.

"Durrr! No, but it will be," Kenny said.

We spent a few more minutes arguing about the rights and wrongs of the idea until I said, "Look, we're only *borrowing* the bike. She'll get it back. The important thing is it'll give the rest of you chance to sneak in and rescue Bubbles."

"I don't know," Lyndz said, still not at all sure about it. "Borrowing Emma Hughes' bike is one thing, *breaking and entering* is another."

"I think Lyndz is right," Fliss said, glad of a get-out.

My plan was looking dead in the water and I was feeling really frustrated. But Kenny came to the rescue. 'You get the bike," she said to me. "I'll get the bear."

But I didn't see why the two of us should do it all. I had another idea. We'd already given Rosie a few small initiation tests, but if she was really going to be one of us it was time for her to prove herself.

"I think Rosie should get Bubbles," I said.

The others looked a little shocked, but Rosie didn't miss a beat. "I'm up for it," she said. "Why not?"

"OK then, I'll go with her," Lyndz said reluctantly.

"What about me?" Fliss asked mournfully.

"You can be look-out," I told her, "in case the M&Ms come back unexpectedly."

"What would we do then?" she asked, horror stricken.

"Leg it," Kenny said, "as fast as you can."

Finally we were sorted. Before anyone else could put any more spokes in the wheels of my great bike borrowing plan, Kenny said, "OK, synchronise watches. Let's rendezvous back here at 17:00 hours."

Kenny and I headed off, and the other three

started to follow at a safe distance. We could hear Rosie explaining to Lyndz, who for some weird reason still hasn't learned to tell the time properly, that 17:00 hours was the same as 5 p.m.

"But that only gives us fifteen minutes!" Lyndz said, shocked.

"Bags of time," Kenny called back over her shoulder, but it wasn't really and she suddenly broke into a run. I had to race after her. Even with my long legs, keeping up with Kenny is never easy.

6

Even if I say so myself, this was definitely one of my *best* plans! It all went like clockwork – at least our part did.

When we reached Emily Berryman's house we could see Emma's bike leaning against the side of the garage. I kept lookout while Kenny carefully opened the cast-iron gates and wheeled it out. Then we walked slowly, but confidently, down the road.

"Let's just pretend you're walking home with

me and this is my bike," Kenny suggested to me.

"As *if*," I said. Bright turquoise is far too girly a colour for Kenny.

"I said, *pretend*," Kenny grinned.

As soon as we were round the corner we picked up speed and ran the rest of the way to the small group of shops close to school. We stood the bike outside the newsagents, making sure the owner didn't see us. Mrs Thomas, who's Welsh, is hard of hearing, but she still doesn't miss much.

Then we rang Emily Berryman's number. While it was still ringing I tried to hand Kenny the phone, but she backed off and refused to take it.

"No way," she said. "That's your job."

"Why me?" I said, forcing the phone on her again.

"Because…" she said through gritted teeth, pushing it back at me again, "action's my thing, thinking on your feet and doing silly voices is yours."

Then there was no more time to argue because Emily Berryman was on the other end of the phone, which threw me into a real panic.

"Hello! Hello! Who's there?" she asked.

So I just took a deep breath and launched into this not very convincing Welsh accent, pretending to be Mrs Thomas.

"Is that Emily Berryman?" I yelled into the phone. "I think your friend's bike may have been left outside my shop. It's a very nice turquoise colour. Has she lost a bike like that?"

There was a moment's silence followed by Emily calling out to Emma, "Go look if your bike's still there!"

There was a far-off sound of screaming, then Emily said, "Please don't take your eyes off it. We'll be there in two minutes."

Kenny and I hung around watching over the bike until we saw the M&Ms and Alana Banana turn the corner. Then we ducked behind the chip shop, but peeped out to watch what happened.

We couldn't stop giggling at Mrs Thomas's amazed face when Emma Hughes said gushingly, "Thank you so much for watching my bike, I'm very grateful to you."

Mrs Thomas looked blankly at her, as if she'd misheard.

"I don't suppose you saw who put it there?" Emma asked, shouting this time. But Mrs Thomas shook her head and continued to look confused. They finally gave up and turned to go home; Kenny and I followed at a safe distance.

"Phew! Let's hope that's given the others the time they needed," Kenny said.

I sincerely hoped it had: it had been a bit scary and I wouldn't have wanted to do it all over again. But our part in the plan had been a complete doddle compared to the trouble the others had – mainly thanks to Buster.

Buster is Lyndz's crazy little Jack Russell terrier. As my gran says: he's a law unto himself. Buster won't go on a lead like other dogs and he's always running away, sometimes for hours on end. He always comes back when it's mealtime, though. Another strange habit he has is jumping. It's like he has spring-loaded feet; we sometimes call him Bouncing Buster, the high-jumping dog.

The first couple of times the others tried to set off, Buster had followed them and Lyndz had had to take him back. Finally she locked him in the house and then they hurried round to Emily's house. All according to plan they saw the M&Ms disappearing down the street. Rosie and Lyndz left Fliss to keep watch while they slipped through the side gate, which the M&Ms had thoughtfully left wide open for them.

They quickly checked Emily's mum wasn't at her kitchen window, then Rosie made a dash for Bubbles. What none of us had banked on was that the Gruesome Twosome had tied Bubbles into the chair with a long piece of rope using a few cunning knots we'd learned at Brownies.

Fortunately Rosie has some nails; Lyndz would never have managed on her own because she chews hers right down. Even so it was taking her much longer than they'd expected.

"Let's just take the stupid chair as well," Rosie hissed at Lyndz.

"Absolutely not," Lyndz hissed back. "Breaking

and entering's bad enough. We're not adding daylight robbery to our list of crimes."

While they were still arguing it out they heard a scuffle round the side of the house and Fliss's voice crying out, "Oh, no you don't. You get back here," as Buster shot into view and started racing around Emily's garden like it was some dog's adventure playground he'd just discovered.

Fliss shot in after him but Lyndz ordered her straight back out to take up her post again. Then she started chasing Buster herself.

It must have been a hilarious sight – like a silent movie. They were all so terrified of making a sound and attracting any attention from the house that Lyndz silently chased Buster – while Rosie, hidden from the house by a bush, valiantly fought with the last two double hitch knots.

They were both close to hysterics when they heard Fliss call out, "Oh, no, oh, help! The M&Ms are coming back!"

With one final tug Rosie freed Bubbles. "Yesss!" she hissed in triumph. Then she stuck him under one arm and turned to go. But Buster was suddenly flying towards her, so she made a quick lunge for him with her free hand.

"Come here, you mutt," she gasped as the crazy animal shot through her legs. Buster was hotly pursued by Lyndz, who was running far too fast to stop, and ran smack, bang, wallop into Rosie, almost knocking her out.

"Owwww!" Rosie yelled.

"Owwww, yourself!" Lyndz yelled back.

Rosie described how both of them stood clutching their heads as Buster ran rings round them so fast it made them dizzy to watch him.

In the end Lyndz said wearily, "Just leave him. He thinks it's a game now. If we go he's bound to follow. Come on."

And with that the two of them slipped out by the side gate, leaving Buster to make his own way home. They found Fliss – shaking like a leaf, she told us afterwards – pressed back almost into the hedge. They each grabbed her by a hand and walked with their heads down until they reached the small park, where they broke into a run.

Thankfully, they were pretty sure, the M&Ms hadn't seen them.

With perfect timing, we were all back up in the tree house by 17:00 hours. Fliss gave Bubbles a welcome home hug then we all sat round taking turns to wave him in the air like a trophy. We were feeling pretty excited after our victory, cheering and screaming so much that Lyndz's mum came out to see what on earth was going on.

After she'd gone back in, Kenny leant right out of the tree house again to get a good view of Emily Berryman's garden.

We each grabbed the binoculars in turn to get a quick glimpse of the M&Ms shaking their heads in disbelief and waving their arms around like mad things. We thought it was a bit OTT. After all, they'd stolen our mascot in the first place. What did they expect? That we'd take it all lying down?

We were all laughing and cheering so loudly that at first we didn't hear the racket Buster was making down below.

"Buster! Pack it in!" Lyndz finally called down, but it had no effect.

In the end we looked over the side of the tree house to see what was driving him so crazy.

The mad dog was doing what looked like a victory war dance around something lying at his feet. It was round and brown and looked familiar. When he was sure he'd got our attention Buster stopped yapping and picked up something else brown, but a lot smaller, between his teeth and held it up to us.

Even from that distance we had no trouble recognising it, but Fliss was the one to put it into words: "Oh, my god, he's stolen the M&Ms mascot. *And he's bitten his leg off!*"

We sent Kenny scuttling down the ladder to rescue the bear before Buster could eat any more of his body parts. When she climbed back up and we saw the state of him – and his mangled leg – we knew we were all in deepest doom!

No one knew what to say at first, and then, as

usually happens when we're in trouble, everyone started talking at once.

"Oh, Buster, what have you done?" Lyndz wailed.

"Oh noooo, now what are we going to do?" Fliss groaned.

"Nothing," Kenny announced.

"What do you mean nothing?" Lyndz argued. "We can't do *nothing*!"

"Why not?" said Kenny. "I think it serves them right. They started it all in the first place."

"That's true," said Rosie.

I tended to agree with Kenny, too, although I could see that left us with a bit of a problem to sort out. But before we could discuss it any more Lyndz's mum called up to tell her it was time for tea and that we should all be getting home.

"What happens now?" Fliss hissed at us.

"We'll have to take it back," Lyndz said simply.

"In that state?" Rosie asked.

"Listen," I said, taking control, "we can't do anything now. We'll sleep on it and decide what to do tomorrow."

"Yeah, but what are we going to do with it *now*?" Fliss asked again, her voice rising in panic.

"I don't want it left here," Lyndz said firmly.

Someone had to take it home with them. It would be difficult for Kenny to keep it out of sight, since she shared a bedroom with Molly the Monster. We didn't want to give her any ammunition for getting Kenny in trouble. I didn't *really* want my parents to see it either; I didn't want to have to lie about it. I was already in their bad books.

But Rosie suddenly picked up the bear and stuffed it, and its chewed wet leg, into her bag. "I'll take it," she volunteered. "No probs."

She grinned at us as if it really was no big deal. Despite my reservations about her, even I had to admit that Rosie Cartwright was turning into a bit of a star player.

7

That evening our phones were red hot: I rang Kenny, Kenny rang Lyndz, Lyndz rang me, Fliss rang Lyndz *and* me. But no one was ringing Rosie. We didn't want to find out the evidence had been discovered. (Rosie told us the next morning we needn't have worried. Her house is so big and so disorganised she could have hidden a couple of bodies there and no one would know.)

We were pretty sure the M&Ms would have worked out who'd got their mascot by now. It was bound to blow up into a massive Campaign of Revenge against the whole Sleepover Club. But Fliss was convinced they'd save the worst for her.

"I won't sleep until it's all over," she swore.

The next morning, when the M&Ms overtook us on our way to school, she started muttering under her breath, "Oh-my-god, deepest doom, here I come."

But the M&Ms walked on past and hardly gave us a look. They were deep in conversation with Alana Palmer and judging by her face they were telling her a pretty fascinating story. We felt certain it was about us.

They carried on chatting all through the first lesson and we got to overhear bits when the M&Ms were queuing to speak to Mrs Weaver and leaned on our table.

"Colonel Mustard wasn't just any bear, you know," Emily Berryman told Alana. (*Colonel Mustard?* We couldn't believe that name, but we tried not laugh and give ourselves away.)

"He belonged to my grandma. He was a family heirloom, you know."

"He was incredibly old – and worth *loads* of money," Emma said. "Emily's grandma had him valued once…"

"On Antiques Roadshow…" Emily added.

"They said he could fetch *thousands of pounds*…" Emma continued.

"Maybe more…" Emily corrected her.

"Luckily he was insured," Emma said, turning for the first time to look straight at us. "In fact that was the first thing *the police* asked."

When Fliss heard the word "police" she suddenly squeaked, like she'd turned into a gerbil. Kenny gave her a warning pinch.

"They said they have several leads to follow," Emily said, turning in our direction too. "Apparently the culprits left their fingerprints *all over* the place. It's only a matter of time."

At the words "fingerprints" and "culprits" Fliss gave two little gasps until Kenny stamped on her foot. But this only made Fliss gasp louder and give Kenny an evil look. So I hastily jumped up, announcing that I needed a book from the library corner.

"Come and help me find it," I said, dragging Fliss with me before she did anything else to incriminate herself and the rest of us.

We could hardly wait for break time to hold an emergency meeting. It followed our usual pattern with Kenny and I lining up on one side of the argument and Fliss and Lyndz on the other.

"There's no alternative," Lyndz said. "We just have to own up and take our punishment."

Fliss didn't like the sound of that, but she couldn't see any way around it. "Let's just get it over with, as soon as possible," she groaned, stretching out her arms as if she was ready for the handcuffs.

"Are you crazy?" Kenny asked them. "You can't believe all that rubbish? You saw it. It was just some beat-up old bear of Berryman's."

"We can't be sure about that," said Lyndz. "We only saw it *after* Buster got his teeth into it."

"Even if it's true," Kenny said, "they brought it on themselves. I say we dig a hole, bury the evidence and forget all about it."

"We can't do that," Lyndz said, turning to me, "can we, Frankie?"

Part of me was with Kenny: you simply couldn't believe a word the M&Ms said. "It didn't look like a valuable antique," I agreed.

"It certainly doesn't now," Rosie confirmed. "It's got a big hole in its bottom, as well as a missing leg."

"My mum'll die if I end up in prison," Fliss said dramatically.

"Oh, get a grip!" Kenny told her unsympathetically.

"Look," I said, trying to calm everyone down, "there's got to be a way of putting things right without actually giving ourselves away. We just need a bit of time to come up with it."

But Fliss couldn't wait. She insisted we take a vote there and then between a) those people who favoured coming clean and getting it over with and b) the ostriches who wanted to bury their heads in the sand. She and Lyndz raised their hands for the first option. Kenny and I were no ostriches, but we still voted against them.

Rosie didn't say anything. She just stood there looking awkward and so did the rest of us. If we gave Rosie a vote now it would be like finally making her a full member of the Sleepover Club. I still wasn't sure I was ready for that. On the other hand, with her vote we wouldn't end in stalemate as we usually did. When the others turned to me, I decided to take a risk.

"Well," I asked her, "what side are you on?"

But Rosie didn't take either side; instead she came up with a third option: "Shouldn't we try to repair it first, before we give up and actually admit our part in it?"

"And what if we can't?" Fliss pressed her.

"Then we'll just have to fess up and face the consequences."

This seemed like a compromise we could all live with, which was a good thing because it was time to go back into class.

Today was Wednesday, the quiz was on Friday afternoon. By then, we decided, it had to be sorted – one way or the other.

The one thing we were all agreed on was that we *badly* needed a sleepover. Looking on the worst side and things didn't work out – even if we didn't all end up in jail, as Fliss feared – it could be the last sleepover in the whole history of the Sleepover Club. On the other hand, if things did work out – *and* we won the cup – boy, would we have something to celebrate. It wouldn't be easy to persuade our parents, but we all promised to go home and try an evening of begging and buttering up and see whose parents caved first. I had a feeling it wouldn't be mine. The last lot of trouble was at my house and my parents had memories like elephants.

In the meantime we had to make sure we didn't lose sight of the quiz. We'd had a vote on who should go forward from our team to represent us and everyone agreed it should be Rosie – and me! I realised I couldn't just rely on Rosie being the infallible answering machine. I had to get my act together and start doing my share. We'd all let the M&Ms distract us too much already.

Kenny and I were certain they were just playing mind games with us, and mostly we didn't believe a word the M&Ms were saying. But later that day, when we heard them telling other people in the class about the huge reward that was going to be announced, and saw the Missing Bear poster Emily Berryman was designing – **Have YOU seen Colonel Mustard?** – even we began to wonder whether Fliss was right and we were all headed for jail.

I decided to check the possibility out with Mum and Dad at supper that evening. "Do they ever send children to prison?" I asked lightly.

"Why, what have you done now?" Dad asked immediately.

"Don't be silly," I said, trying to look innocent. "It was a hypothetical question."

"It depends on the crime," Mum said. "If it's serious enough, they might be sent to a young offenders' institution."

"Don't worry," said Dad. "We'd come and visit."

"Yeah," said Mum, "and bring the odd pizza."

"With an iron file in it," Dad said, grinning.

"Very funny," I said. But it wasn't. It was a terrible thought. I was desperate to change the subject.

"I don't suppose there's even the *teeny-weeniest* chance you'd let us have a sleepover this weekend, if I was especially good and helpful and perfect in every way, shape and form?" I asked, giving them my most appealing smile.

It wasn't too successful. Dad looked me right in the eye and said nothing.

"On a scale of one to ten?" I wittered on, still hopeful.

"After the last time?" Dad asked, definitely not smiling. "I'd say… minus ten."

"And a half," said Mum.

"I'll take that as a no, then," I said.

I was disappointed but I can't say I was surprised.

The next day when we compared notes we'd all had the same amount of luck: zero. Lyndz said she hadn't given up on her parents, though. It was still a long shot, but she'd keep working on them.

The M&Ms were playing it dead cool. They still hadn't actually accused us of taking their mascot.

"Maybe they don't *know* it was us," said Fliss. "Maybe they think there really *was* a break-in."

Lyndz pointed out that there really *was* a break-in, and that she and Rosie had done it.

"I was there as well," Fliss moaned, "*at the scene of the crime.*"

"Oh, calm down," Kenny told everyone. "They can't have any proof, or they'd have snitched to Mrs Weaver by now."

"If they tell her they know it was us because we stole Bubbles back," I pointed out, "they'd have to admit they'd stolen him in the first place."

"She's got a point," Rosie said. "They can't tell on us any more than we can tell on them," which was some comfort anyway.

83

But Lyndz reminded us we were running out of time. "The quiz is tomorrow and we agreed the bear had to be repaired and returned by then."

"I'll need some help in that case," Rosie said. "I can't do it on my own, as well as practising for tomorrow."

Rosie had agreed to come to my house for a final cramming session. Kenny had athletics training and Lyndz had to help her mum. But Fliss volunteered to help with Colonel Mustard's leg.

"Call at mine on your way to Frankie's," she told Rosie. "I'll give you a hand."

Rosie nodded. She looked a bit stressed. None of us were feeling exactly confident any more. But if we were getting worried, so were the M&Ms.

All morning we'd noticed them trying to suck up to the teacher, offering to do jobs for her. During the lunch hour, after everyone else had gone to eat, they were still hanging around like a bad smell. So we hung back too, to listen in. We could hardly believe our ears. It only confirmed what I've always suspected about those two creeping-crawlers: they probably manage to win as often as they do – by cheating.

"Now you know I can't tell you that, Emma," Mrs Weaver said, laughing.

"Not even one or two of the subjects?" Emma asked, batting her eyelids.

"Not even the subjects, no. Really, girls, that would be very unsportsman-like."

As if the M&Ms cared about that. All they cared about was winning that cup and they would stop at nothing.

But even by *their* standards their next tactic was pretty low: divide and rule. And guess who they picked as their target.

Thursday's always a busy night because everyone does different after-school activities. It's the one night we don't all walk home together. Rosie lives a bit out of our way in any case, so she headed off alone.

The first clue that anything was wrong was when she didn't show up at Fliss's as she'd promised. Fliss rang to find out where she was and got Rosie's sister Tiff on the phone.

"She's not coming and she doesn't want to speak to you!" Tiff said.

Fliss rang me straightaway. "What did I do?" she wailed down the phone.

I didn't know, but I was going to find out. When I rang I got the same message from Tiff. And, no, there was no explanation.

Something funny was going on and we needed to get to the bottom of it. I didn't think I was the best person to sort it out, but I knew who was.

"Lyndz, get on your bike and go round to Rosie's house," I told her. Pronto."

"Now? I can't," she said in between licking something and making yummy noises. "I'm helping Mum make blackberry jam."

"Listen!" I told her. "Never mind blackberry jam. We have an emergency!"

When she got to Rosie's, Lyndz got the same brick wall treatment from Tiff, but that didn't stop her.

"Please tell Rosie I'm going to camp out on the doorstep until she comes out to talk to me," she said, and she meant it. Lyndz can be pretty tough when she sets her mind to something. She's also great at winkling things out of people. In the end she got the whole story.

When Rosie left school she hadn't gone far before she found the M&Ms waiting for her. They pretended to be really friendly at first, asking her how she was liking the area, the school, *the people*... Then they told her this whole pack of lies about us: about how we always pretend to be nice to people until we've got what we want out of them – like winning the Weakest Link – then we drop them like a brick.

"They never planned to let you join the Sleepover Club," they told her, "they're just using you."

"To get that cup," Emily said.

"That's the kind of people they are," Emma Hughes told her, "especially that football-mad Kenny and that weirdo Frankie."

"Surely you realised that?" Emily said.

"We couldn't work out why a nice, intelligent person like you would want to hang out with a bunch of losers and users like them," Emma told her, "when you could be hanging out with us!"

Lyndz didn't have to say anything, because as Rosie told the story she began to realise for herself how the Gruesome Twosome had set her up.

"I'm really sorry," she said. "I don't know what made me listen to them."

"You don't have to apologise to me," Lyndz said. "We should probably have warned you just how evil those two can be."

But by the time it was all sorted it was far too late for Rosie to do any mending with Fliss, or cramming for tomorrow with me.

Lyndz rang me as soon as she got home. "Listen, Frankie, Rosie looked really down when I left. I don't think she's going to be her best tomorrow so *you'd* better be in a good place."

"Oh, gee, thanks, Lyndz," I said. "No pressure then."

Afterwards I felt so freaked with the responsibility I stayed up far too late cramming in more facts than my brain had space for, which wasn't the cleverest thing I could have done.

And Rosie felt so bad about even listening to those muppets, especially after we all sent her texts telling her we really were her friends, that she stayed up too late, too, trying to mend the bear all on her own.

By Friday morning our team couldn't have looked in much worse shape. Everyone else in our class was feeling excited, waving their mascots and firing random questions at each other, trying to guess what Mrs Weaver might ask. But we all sat round our table with our heads in our hands, wondering if it was worth bothering.

"We haven't even got a mascot for luck," Fliss complained. Although we'd got Bubbles back, we couldn't possibly use him, because if we did it'd be like admitting to the M&Ms we'd gone into Emily's garden and rescued him. And we all agreed it seemed disloyal to Bubbles to have any other mascot.

But we certainly needed something to bring us luck and raise our spirits. Especially after Rosie showed us what kind of a job she'd made of Colonel Mustard's leg – and the hole in his bottom. At that point any hopes we had that we could avoid having to own up to our crimes and what Buster had done finally disappeared.

"I'm sorry, it's the best I could do," Rosie said apologetically.

Kenny still insisted it was clearly just some beat-up old bear. But that hardly mattered any more. Even if the police story was made up, the bear was still someone else's property. We were going to have to come clean at some point and putting it off was just making us more miserable. But the thought of looking at the M&Ms' smug faces convinced us to put it off a little longer… at least until lunchtime.

It seemed as if the lower we sank the happier the M&Ms got. They'd been swaggering around the classroom all morning as if they'd already won. When they finally did, which we thought was pretty inevitable now, we knew they'd be completely UNBEARABLE.

In an otherwise dreadful day there was one glimmer of hope: Lyndz's parents had offered her a deal.

"What sort of deal?" Kenny asked.

"We *can* have a sleepover at mine this weekend…" she said.

"What's the catch?" I asked, because I could tell there was one coming.

"*If* our team wins *The Weakest Link*."

"Is that all?" Kenny said cheerfully.

"I told Dad that's called bribery," Lyndz said. "But he said, it's called 'incentive'."

"It's called the final straw," I groaned. Now even our sleepover rested on Rosie and me.

"You can do it," Kenny said, slapping me on the back.

"You've *got* to do it," Fliss said, almost pleading with us.

Even Lyndz piled on more pressure when she said, "We're all depending on you two," as if we didn't already know that.

"At least things can't get any worse," Rosie whispered to me as we went back into class.

But she was wrong – they could and they did.

The next lesson was art, which at least meant we could switch off and sit together in a huddle feeling sorry for ourselves.

Lyndz cheered herself up doing this brilliant picture of a horse and a foal. She looked really proud of it as she turned it round to show me.

"Wow, Lyndz, that's mega."

But just at that point Kenny and Fliss reached for the same paint pot. It splattered Kenny's Leicester City Football top and then poured a stream of paint right across Lyndz's picture.

"Oh, Kenny!" Lyndz wailed and gave Kenny a really hurt look.

"It wasn't *my* fault," Kenny growled and gave Fliss a murderous look.

"Don't blame *me*!" Fliss growled and glared back at Kenny.

"Uh-oh," Rosie whispered under her breath to me.

Fortunately before World War Three broke out Mrs Weaver came over and said, "Quickly, Kenny, go and get it washed off before it stains."

Kenny went off to the toilets while I sympathised with Lyndz – her picture was completely ruined – and Rosie tried to reassure Fliss it hadn't been her fault.

Now we were even falling out between ourselves and I blamed it all on the M&Ms. I was so mad with them I just wanted to go over and give them their stupid bear back, over their stupid heads. I'd have done if too if they hadn't suddenly disappeared.

Kenny is so proud of her football tops. I was dreading her coming back from the toilets if the paint hadn't come out. But when she did she was wearing her spare PE shirt and the biggest grin on her face you ever saw.

"What's with you?" I asked.

"I have just overheard the most *interesting* conversation..." she grinned "...between the M&Ms."

We all crowded round as she reported it back to us. Within minutes we were completely united again and looking for serious payback.

Kenny told us, "I was in one of the cubicles getting changed when the gruesome M&Ms came in laughing about how easily they'd tricked us. I told you that bear wasn't antique! It wasn't precious at all; it was just some old beat-up one of Berryman's, like I said. The little liar said it was worth losing, if it meant getting one over on *the idiotic Sleepover Club*."

Idiotic! Us? Now they were seriously asking for trouble. But Kenny hadn't finished yet. Next she told us that Emma Hughes had said, "I knew they'd fall for it, especially that Slidebottom dummy."

"Have you seen how sick they're all looking this morning?" Emily had agreed.

"Winning *The Weakest Link* is going to be a piece of cake now."

"Then our revenge will be complete."

"Dummy! They called *me* a dummy?" Fliss started to hyperventilate. "Those insects are going to pay for this," she hissed.

"We're going to stamp on them," Rosie agreed.

"Grind them into the ground," Kenny added.

"Wipe them off the face of the planet," Lyndz rounded off.

At lunchtime we had another emergency meeting. Kenny wanted to go and confront the M&Ms and let them know we were finally on to them. But I had a better idea.

"If we let them go on thinking they've put one over on us, we go into the quiz with a big advantage," I said. "Now that we know it was all a trick and we don't have to worry about their stupid bear, we can just concentrate on winning."

"Yeah," Rosie agreed, "that will be the best payback."

And I had another little idea to unnerve

those two slugs. It also gave Kenny a chance to use up a bit of her anger and excess energy. I sent her racing round to Fliss's house on Lyndz's bike to bring back Bubbles.

"Bubbles?" Fliss said surprised.

"That's right," I smiled. There was no need to pretend any more. From now on it was all-out, no holds barred, full-on warfare – and we were going to win.

Mrs Weaver had been busy all lunch hour setting up the small hall for the quiz. Even though Rosie and I were a mess of nerves we felt really excited when we saw it. There were twelve places each marked with our names set out in a semicircle, just like on TV. We each had a plastic board and a marker pen to vote someone off at the end of each round. Before we started Mrs Weaver went through the rules with the twelve of us and explained how it would work.

Then the rest of the class came in and sat round on the floor and Mrs Weaver took her place in the middle of the room with the questions. Our teacher doesn't look a bit bad-tempered like Anne Robinson, and she doesn't wear glasses, but today she put on a heavy dark pair and tried to make herself frown, which just made everyone laugh. But it got us all off to a good start.

"Welcome to *The Weakest Link*," she said. "Anyone here could win this cup, the rest will leave with... nothing. There are twelve contestants..." and then we had to go round and say our names.

Then Mrs Weaver said, "It's time to play... *The Weakest Link*." And we all got started.

In the first round the questions were easy-peasy, but even so Danny McCloud didn't get a single one right. The whole time he was fooling about, so he was the first to get voted off. His name was on everyone's board.

"You are the Weakest Link," Mrs Weaver

said. "Goodbye." And she looked quite glad to see the back of him.

At the end of the next round, Mrs Weaver said, "So, whose train has run out of steam, who's heading for the sidings? It's time to reveal the Weakest Link," and even though we knew Fliss would probably never speak to us again both Rosie and I chose Ryan Scott. When he did his walk of shame half the girls in the class looked close to tears.

With each round the questions got harder and by the time we'd reached Round Six both Rosie and I were having to really concentrate. By now there were six of us left: us two, the Gruesome Twosome, Regina Hill and a nerdy boy, called Shaun Stokes.

He was unlucky because he got two questions about sport and pop music, two things he said he knows nothing about. So he went out next.

Even though neither Rosie nor I had been getting many questions wrong, the M&Ms kept trying to vote one of us off. Fortunately no one else had agreed with them – so far we were both saved.

Emily Berryman had got a few questions wrong herself and at the end of Round Seven when Mrs Weaver said, "Who hasn't put a foot right? Who's completely out of step? Who needs chopping off at the knees?" Emily was voted off and I almost cheered. Fliss did cheer, but Lyndz put her hand over her mouth before Mrs Weaver heard her.

"Let's leave that kind of unsportsman-like behaviour to the M&Ms," Lyndz told Fliss. But inside we were all delighted.

I couldn't afford to feel smug for long, though. In Round Eight things started to go wrong for me.

"Frankie," Mrs Weaver asked, "who was the first man to fly in space?"

Phew, I thought, *I know this*. But I didn't.

"Neil Armstrong," I said, stupidly mixing him up with the first man on the moon.

"No, I'm afraid it was Yuri Gagarin."

Emma Hughes gave me such a superior smile, which made me feel even worse when I got the next one wrong too!

"Who was the first wife of Henry the Eighth?"

My mind went a complete blank. I knew his second wife was Anne Boleyn, but could I remember the first! In the end I just had to pass.

So, when Mrs Weaver said, "Who's weighing everyone down? Who's excess baggage. Who is the Weakest Link?" I was certain it would be the end of me.

The votes, though, were completely divided: Emma Hughes and Regina Hill chose me, Rosie and I chose Emma, who'd also got one question wrong. But because I'd got two wrong, I *was* the Weakest Link and had to go. I felt bad for myself, but I felt worse about leaving Rosie on her own to do battle with that big head, Emma Hughes. I tried not to look at her smug mug as I did the Walk of Shame.

Rosie got through Round Nine but at the

end had to make the hard decision of who to vote off. She knew that, even though she had got hardly any questions wrong, if Emma and Regina both voted against her she would still end up the Weakest Link. But if just one of them voted against the other one Rosie could end up staying in. But which should she choose? She dithered so long that Mrs Weaver had to ask her three times for her vote. In the end she held up her board with Regina's name on it, which was the right choice because Emma Hughes had voted her off too. None of us could understand that, but afterwards Rosie said she had a feeling that Emma liked the idea of it being a final fight to the death between them and us.

"That leaves Emma and Rosie to go *head to head*!" Mrs Weaver announced. "I don't know about the rest of you, but the suspense is getting almost too much for me. I suggest we take a break here and come back in fifteen minutes for the final showdown."

We all gathered around poor old Rosie who was looking really sick. All our hopes were resting on her shoulders now. I couldn't do anything else to help, but at least I'd saved our one little extra piece of ammunition for now.

"Time to get Bubbles out," I told Fliss. "At least he might wipe the smile off Emma Hughes' face."

While everyone was filing back in and the last two took their places Rosie held Bubbles proudly in front of her.

We were all watching Emma Hughes' face. Her mouth went all tight – as my grandma says: like she'd been sucking lemons. She wasn't looking so smug any more.

Eventually, in the final head to head they'd had three questions each and the score was three all.

"Because there's a tie," Mrs Weaver explained, "we shall go for sudden death. The first person to give a correct answer wins."

Rosie had gone first, so she had an advantage now. We all had our fingers so tightly crossed we were losing the feeling in them. You could have heard a pin drop in the room.

"Rosie, how do you describe a volcano that has not erupted for a long period?"

Rosie didn't rush it, but she answered quite quickly, "Extinct?" She looked like she had her own doubts about it, even though the rest of us were sure she was right.

But Mrs Weaver said, "No-o-o, *extinct* describes a volcano that is never expected to erupt again. The answer is *dormant*, which means, Emma, if you get this question right you'll be the winner."

We couldn't believe it. Emma Hughes started to look as if it was almost in the bag. She didn't exactly smile, but she was looking pretty sure of herself.

"So, Emma, who is believed to be the richest woman in the world?"

Emma looked like she was sure this was some kind of a trick question. She looked around the room as if someone there could give her the answer, but Emily Berryman was looking as puzzled as the rest of us. In the end Emma shrugged and said, "J.K. Rowling?"

Everyone laughed at that, although it sounded as if it might be true.

"No," Mrs Weaver smiled, "not quite. The answer is: Queen Elizabeth the Second. So, Rosie, you have another chance. This is a really tough one: If *swarm* is the collective noun for bees, what is the collective noun for rattlesnakes?"

Oh, for goodness sake, everyone groaned. Rattlesnakes, honestly, how could Mrs Weaver expect us to know something like that? *Even Rosie won't get that one*, I thought. But how wrong can you be?

Rosie frowned and screwed up her forehead as if she was dragging the answer from the very depths of her brain. Finally she said, "Is it a rhumba of rattlesnakes?"

Everyone burst out laughing, as if it was the silliest answer in the world. But they soon stopped when Mrs Weaver said, "Correct!

Rosie, you are the winner and the Strongest Link. Today you go home with the cup. Emma, you go home... with nothing."

We all cheered and clapped until our hands ached. When Mrs Weaver presented our team with the cup the M&Ms looked fit to explode.

Afterwards Rosie asked them, "Whatever happened to *your* mascot?" and when they glared at her she added, "Oh, maybe he doesn't like hanging out with *losers*!"

"You haven't heard the end of this!" Emma Hughes spluttered.

That we had won the cup was *brilliant*, that we had had our revenge on the M&Ms was *fantabuloso*, that we now had a sleepover to look forward to was the cherry, nuts and double-cream topping on the Knickerbocker Glory.

10

We all arrived at Lyndz's on Saturday night ready to seriously celebrate. Even Buster was excited. All four feet left the ground as he bounced round, his tail wagging fit to fall off. I thought it was because he was pleased to see us, but Lyndz said he could smell Kenny's bag. She and Fliss had both brought Buster presents to reward him for his part in our triumph over the M&Ms. Kenny had brought him a bone; Fliss had made him a little paper chain of teddies to wear round his neck. In minutes he'd eaten both.

While we were still making a fuss of Buster the phone rang. It was the dreaded M&Ms. Now how did they know we were at Lyndz's?

"You don't suppose they could be spying on us?" Fliss said, immediately fussing with her hair and straightening her clothes as if she was on camera.

"You mean a bit like we spied on them?" I reminded her.

"It's a creepy thought," Kenny said, looking over her shoulder.

When Lyndz came back from the phone she said they'd sent us a message: "We want that bear back NOW, and in the exact place it was stolen from. Or we tell the police."

"I told them we were busy having a sleepover," Lyndz added, "but they said, 'That's your problem, *mate*!'"

Well, there was no way we were going round there to walk into some booby trap they'd probably prepared for us. Just thinking about those two was starting to cast a cloud over our sleepover, but Kenny suddenly had this brain wave – a final piece of payback, she called it.

I've told you Kenny has this crazy streak sometimes. Suddenly we all felt like running for cover because we recognised that mad glint in her eye now. But we didn't run; instead we followed her out into Lyndz's garden.

Because Lyndz's dad is always doing DIY and her brothers like messing around with bits of cars, her garden is littered with useful pieces of junk. Kenny pounced on an old car tyre inner tube and muttered darkly, "They want their old bear back, they can have him. In fact, they're going to get him faster than they expected."

"Maybe we should leave it till tomorrow," Lyndz suggested nervously.

"Yeah, let's get on with the sleepover," Fliss almost pleaded.

But Kenny was on a mission. "Who's got the bear?" she asked. When Rosie handed it over, Kenny climbed up into the tree house and reluctantly the rest of us followed her.

It wasn't dark yet, but it was almost dusk. Fliss made the usual fuss; I just swallowed hard and climbed up after her.

When Kenny checked with the binoculars, sure enough the M&Ms were in Emily Berryman's garden, messing around with bits of rope. If they thought we were going to walk into that lion's den they were very much mistaken.

Kenny organised us into our places with Rosie and me at the front, each holding one end of the inner tube, as she explained her Master Plan.

Even by Kenny's standards this was a hairy-scary scheme, but it was absolutely wicked.

"We're going to catapult him through the air, over the dog park, smack, bang, wallop into Emily Berryman's garden," she announced grandly.

"But it's miles away. It'll never work," Fliss insisted.

"Have a little faith," Kenny told her. "It's no distance at all – as the bear flies," she grinned. "And with a bit of luck, and good judgement, if it's exactly on target, it'll hit one of those gonks bang on the head."

Rosie and I thought it was a brilliant idea and well worth a try, but soft-hearted Lyndz took some persuading. As you'd expect she was thinking about the poor old Colonel. In the end Kenny delayed blast-off for ten minutes while Lyndz made him a little parachute out of an old pillowcase to spare him a crash landing.

Finally, Rosie and I braced ourselves while Kenny stretched the inner tube to its full capacity; Fliss and Lyndz stood ready to insert the bear. I was a little worried that if Kenny got too enthusiastic when she fired the bear, we might all be catapulted after him and end up a heap of broken bones in Lyndz's garden. The others were having doubts too.

"Are you sure about this?" Lyndz asked one last time. But Kenny told her with perfect confidence that everything was *totally under control*.

"Ready for countdown!" she began. "Ten –

nine – eight – seven – six – five – four – three – two – one… blast-off!"

You should have seen him go! Just like a rocket being launched from Cape Canaveral.

"Houston, we have lift off!" Kenny announced. Everyone cheered – for about ten seconds – until calamity hit.

As Kenny argued later, if it hadn't been for that sudden gust of wind carrying him off course and into the branches of the big oak tree on the dog park, he would definitely have hit the target. Instead Colonel Mustard hung by his parachute halfway up the tree, gently blowing in the wind

"Oh, Kenny, do something!" Fliss squealed, as if Kenny could launch herself like Superman after him and unhook the bear.

"If you hadn't insisted on that parachute…" Kenny turned on Lyndz.

"If you hadn't come up with such a hair-brained scheme in the first place…" Lyndz rounded on Kenny.

 113

But Rosie and I just looked at each other and started to laugh, and soon all the others were laughing too. In fact, Lyndz's mum had to call three times before we heard her.

"*Girls!* Food's ready. Come on in, it's getting dark."

"Food, yippee!" Kenny yelled and raced down the ladder. As Rosie and Fliss followed her I looked at Lyndz's sad face.

"We can't leave him there, Frankie," she whispered. "We've got to rescue him."

"We will – tomorrow," I promised.

"But how?" she asked.

"Don't worry, I'll think of a way." Me and my big mouth!

11

Lyndz's mum makes the best burgers in the world – meat for the carnivores like Kenny and veggie for me and Lyndz – with fries, and homemade trifle for pudding.

All the time we were eating we tried not to think about the Colonel swinging by his pillowcase parachute from the tree, because whenever one of us did Rosie would start to giggle, which just started everyone else off. I think Lyndz's mum and dad thought we'd all had a silly pill.

By the time we went upstairs we were all ready for a really mad half hour. Kenny suggested one of our Teddy Wrestling Contests.

"Bring it on!" I said, with complete confidence.

My bear Stanley is the undisputed champion and he was ready to take on anything.

"Do we have to?" Fliss asked, less than enthusiastically.

Like I said, Fliss is pretty fearless on her own account, but she doesn't like to see her toys taking a beating, so Bubbles quickly conceded defeat. He sat watching the rest, wearing his Strongest Link sash and a little matching crown Fliss had made him that said *WINNER* on it.

The rest of us battled it out and the final was between Stanley and Rosie's bear, Dougal.

Rosie and I held our bears out and eyeballed each other. I smiled menacingly and asked, "Ready for a humiliating defeat?"

"If you think you're ready to take on the strongest link?" she reminded me.

But this was a pure test of strength.

Wrestlers didn't need to know about *rhumbas of rattlesnakes* I reminded her and in no time Dougal was retiring from the ring. I finally sat Stanley beside Bubbles wearing his Champion Wrestler's cloak.

They looked such a funny pair: big, tough Stanley and little pink Bubbles, but then when I looked around the room we looked a bit of an odd mixture too.

I'd been thinking a lot lately about what makes the Sleepover Club so special and I decided that was it: that we we're all the very best of friends and yet as different as five girls could be.

Kenny is… well, Kenny, there's no one quite like her. She's crazy, but in a good way, and a real energy machine. Plus she pulls the worst – which means the best – ugly faces in the world. She has us all in hysterics.

Lyndz is kindness on legs. She can be very funny too, especially when she gets hiccups, which is often. She's the one who keeps us all on the right path when we start to go a bit haywire.

Fliss is probably the funniest of all even though she often doesn't realise it. She's fierce and loyal and although she's not the bravest person in the world she really tries to be, which I think is the best kind of bravery. I know we tease her all the time, but we all agree the club just wouldn't be the same without her.

And, although I'm not one to blow my own trumpet… No, really, I'm not… I'm the one who gets things organised and has the bright ideas. Far too many ideas, my mum and dad are always telling me. So I suppose you'd say I'm the leader, but probably best not tell Fliss that.

And now there's Rosie, too.

What I've learned this week is that although I don't really like change, sometimes it *can* be for the better – like Rosie joining the club. She absolutely felt like one of us by now and this seemed like the right time to make it official.

Once we were all in our PJs sitting in the circle, I handed Rosie a little package. She went all pink when she saw it.

"Open it! Open it!" the others chanted.

Inside was Rosie's Sleepover Club membership card. She didn't say anything – I think she suddenly felt a bit shy – she just grinned at us and we grinned back at her. As well as her membership card there was a friendship fan I'd organised earlier. We'd all written on it the things we already knew and loved about Rosie: that she's clever – she'd certainly proved that this week – funny and brave and pretty cool. When she read them out loud she went even pinker.

It was far too embarrassing for Kenny who can't bear what she calls "that soppy stuff". She stood on her head and made monkey noises, which was the signal for a second mad half hour with squishy poohs.

Later, when we were sitting having our midnight feast, Rosie suddenly asked, "What is it with you lot and cucumber?"

So I told her how at one of our first sleepovers Fliss had tried to give us all beauty treatments and made us lie on the floor with slices of cucumber on our eyelids – "to refresh the skin", she'd said. But Kenny had got bored and eaten hers and then felt peckish and had gone round lifting them off and scoffing everyone else's.

"Ever since then we *always* have to have cucumber in our midnight feasts."

"It's a Sleepover Club thing," Kenny said, sticking out her tongue and revealing a thin ring of cucumber on it.

"I was right," Rosie shrugged. "You really are *weird.*"

"You think that's weird?" Kenny asked her menacingly. "We'll show you weird…" and we all advanced on her like a pack of zombies, then piled on top of her and tickled her until she begged for mercy.

"OK, OK, sorry," she squealed. "You're not weird… you're…" We let her up for air until she got out the next words "…absolutely barking mad," and we piled in again.

I don't think her opinion changed much

when we taught her our Sleepover Club song and the hand movements to go with it:

Down by the river there's a hanky-pankyyy,
With a bullfrog sitting near the hanky-pankyyy.
With an ooh-ah, ooh-ah…
Hey, Mrs Zippy, with a 1-2-3 OUT!

What we hadn't told Rosie was that at the end we each try to be the first to lie down and turn off our torches, leaving the last person – *her* – sitting up in the dark on her own, feeling a bit *creepy*.

"Aaargh!" she squealed, then muttered almost to herself, "Did I say barking mad? I should have said *totally bonkers*."

So that was it – payback a third time – and this time she didn't see us coming! *Aaaahhhh!*

When we were finally lying in our sleeping bags all lined up on the floor in Lyndz's bedroom we still didn't want to go to sleep. So we did a round of Share a Secret. I went last and when it came to me I decided to be really honest like my parents always tell me to be. Have you noticed how it somehow feels easier to say things in the dark?

"At first I didn't really want Rosie to join the Sleepover Club," I told them. I heard Fliss draw in her breath, and the others went completely silent, waiting to see what I was going to say next. "But I was so wrong about that. It was the best thing that's happened since the night we first started. It feels like she really belongs. In fact, she's the extra link that's made us even stronger."

No one said anything; they didn't need to. That's what it's like between best friends. Sometimes you just know what each other's thinking. You don't always have to say it.

So that's the whole story: the how, when and why of the Sleepover Club. If you hang round a bit longer the others will be here and you can help us sort out the latest fine mess Kenny got us into. Although I'm not really blaming Kenny; we were all in it together.

I suppose I'd have to admit we all get a bit carried away sometimes and do things we aren't always proud of afterwards. You know, things you wouldn't want other people to know about. But we usually try to put things right in the end.

Anyway, I've worked out a plan for when they come. We're going to have to make a pyramid, so we can get Kenny high enough to reach the lower branches. After that she'll be up that tree like a monkey.

Yes, I did say Kenny. Well, I'm not going up there, am I? It's like Kenny said: we all have our strengths and action is hers.

But, listen, the others don't need to know about heights not being mine. It'll just be our secret, OK?

Here they come now. Wish us luck, because if things don't go to plan this time it really will be perpetual doom – for all of us.

Remember, not a word to the others about you know what and you'll be my friend forever.

Top SleePOVer TIPS

Membership Cards

Make your own club official with this guide to making membership cards!

The SleePOVer Club Membership Card

Name: Frankie

Date of Birth: 29th April 1997

Signature: Frankie

You will need:

Card
Passport photo of you
Sticky-back plastic
Scissors (take care)
Glue (PVA or Pritt Stick)
Pens and felt tips
Ruler

Now the instructions!

1 Using my sleepover membership card as a guide, cut out a rectangular piece of card a similar size.

2 Using a pen and a ruler, add sections for your name, date of birth and signature, leaving a space on the left for your passport photo. Fill in your details and sign your best signature.

3 Draw your own club logo on to the membership card (if you have one), if not use ours!

4 Trim your passport photo to fit and glue it to the space on the left.

5 Cut a piece of sticky-back plastic the same shape but slightly bigger than your membership card. Peel off the backing and stick it over the front of your card to protect your artwork and photo.

6 Cut slits in the corners of the overlapping sticky-back plastic and stick it down neatly to the reverse side of your card.

Frankie x

Frankie's Friendly Feast!

These dip recipes are
great for sharing with
your besties!

Cheese & Chives

You will need:

- Carrots
- Cucumber
- Tortilla chips or your
  favourite crisps
- 3 tablespoons of half fat crème
  fraiche or fromage frais
- 2 tablespoons grated cheese
- Handful of chopped chives
- Black pepper

1. Mix together the crème fraiche/fromage
   frais, grated cheese and chives and add
   pepper to taste.

2. Cut carrots and cucumber into baton
   shapes.

3. Open your crisps and get dipping!

Top Choc Dip

You will need:

- Your favourite chocolate bar
  (one bar will serve two people,
  so you may need few)
- Cocktail sticks
- Strawberries
- Grapes
- Marshmallows

ASK AN ADULT FOR HELP!

1 Break the chocolate bar into chunks and put them in a microwave proof bowl.

2 Cook for 1 minute on a medium heat then stir.

3 Cook for another 30 seconds if necessary.

4 Wait a couple of minutes – until the chocolate is cool enough to eat, but gooey enough to dip.

5 Skewer the fruit and marshmallows on cocktail sticks and get dipping!

Frankie x

YOU are invited to join Frankie, Fliss, Kenny, Rosie and me for our next sleepover in...

TV

The Sleepover Club

Stars!

When Fliss persuaded us to come to her audition, we all got into the acting groove! Time to climb our way up the celeb ladder!

Are **you** set for stardom?
Come along and join the club!

From *Lyndz* ✗